DATE

Don't Drag Your Feet...

story & pictures by J O S E P H   L O W

A Margaret K. McElderry Book

ATHENEUM   1983   NEW YORK

For all Tedderfrens

LIBRARY OF CONGRESS CATALOGING IN PUBLICATION DATA

LOW, JOSEPH.
DON'T DRAG YOUR FEET.

"A MARGARET K. MCELDERRY BOOK."
SUMMARY: PEGGY DOESN'T TALK VERY NICELY TO HER TOYS
UNTIL ONE DAY SHE DREAMS THAT THEY ARE BIG AND SHE IS
SMALL AND THEY CAN TALK BUT SHE CANNOT.
[1. TOYS—FICTION. 2. DREAMS—FICTION] I. TITLE.
PZ7.L9598DO 1983 [E] 82-13898
ISBN 0-689-50271-0

PUBLISHED SIMULTANEOUSLY IN CANADA BY MCCLELLAND & STEWART, LTD.
COMPOSITION BY DIX TYPE INC., SYRACUSE, NEW YORK
PRINTED AND BOUND BY HALLIDAY LITHOGRAPH COMPANY, INC.
WEST HANOVER, MASSACHUSETTS
FIRST EDITION

PEGGY wished her toys could talk.

*Did you have
a nice nap,
Froggy?*

*Now then, Lion,
your lovely eye
needs polishing.*

*Mouseykins,
how do you manage
always to get your
dress on backwards?*

*You have crumbs
in your feathers again,
Rooster.*

They never answered her.

Her favorite was a worn old teddybear.

My nice Tedder.

But Tedder never said a word.

No matter what they did

Look at the flowers,
Tedder.

or where they went.

Don't drag
your feet,
Tedder.

Sometimes Peggy was very annoyed.

*Tedder,
you are so
dumb!*

One day when Peggy took her nap
she had a dream.
The world had changed.

What then?

*Well,
I said to
him . . .*

She was small and
the toys were big.
And they could talk.

I was
magnificent!

They talked to each other
as if she could not hear them.

Sit up straight, Peggy!

When they talked to Peggy,

they were very bossy.

But *she* couldn't talk!

And they did not make much sense.

Don't interrupt
when I'm talking, Peggy.

Peggy had not said a word.

You just
aren't <u>trying</u>,
Peggy!

Rooster insisted

Peggy must learn to fly.

Mousey jammed
some shoes on
Peggy, but they were
too big and on the
wrong feet.

Lion made her
take a nap in
broad daylight.
She had to
close her eyes.
She had to
pretend to be
asleep to stop
his fussing.

You <u>need</u>
to take a nap, Peggy.

Tedder took Peggy for a walk.
But he wouldn't let her stop
to look at the flowers.

Don't dawdle,
Peggy.

Or the pretty butterflies.

Nasty bugs!

Do your little dance for nice
Mr. Duckwaddle.

Tedder made her be polite.

When Peggy was too tired to walk,
Tedder dragged her.

*How could you be so
careless, Peggy?*

She fell in a puddle and Tedder shook her
hard to get the water off.

He was angry,
but it was he
who had got her
into the puddle.

Tedder hung her
on the branch of a tree.

How she wished someone
would be nice to her!

Stay there
until you're dry.

Along came a big dog.

He didn't say anything.
He just took Peggy's dress in
his soft mouth and carried her away.

Peggy was surprised.
She enjoyed the ride.
Whenever she wanted
to look at a flower,
Big Dog would gently
put her down.

When Peggy was ready to
go on again, Big Dog
picked her up.
They were happy
together.

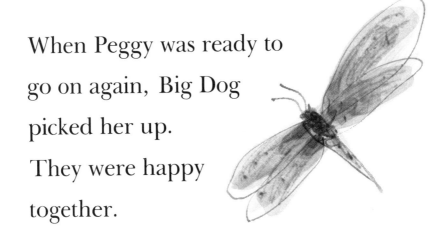

They were happy until
Tedder caught up with them.
Tedder was very angry!

Peggy fell through a cloud.

It was dark and wet
inside the cloud,
but she came out
into the sun again.

A big bird caught
her dress in his beak.

The bird flew to the top of a tree
and put Peggy in his nest.

Then he flew away.

Stay!

When he came back, he had a bug in his beak.

He tried to make Peggy eat the bug.

Peggy ran round and round the nest

to get away from it.

She tripped over the edge of the nest.
As she fell, she grabbed a leaf.

Down and

down she fell,

but not too fast.

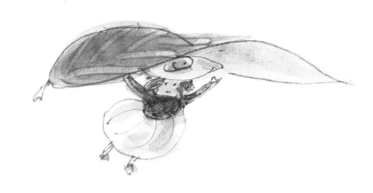

It seemed like floating.

She passed a man in a little airplane.

She floated toward a tall building.

Peggy forgot she was
falling. She just held
tight to her leaf
and looked into
the windows of
the building.

She saw this . . .

and this . . .

and this . . .

and this.

But Peggy *was* falling!

She hit the floor with a bump—

and woke up.

Peggy looked around.

She was back in
her own room again,
and she was the right size.

Her toys were not big.
They were just their old,
familiar selves.

Peggy ran over and took Tedder
out of the toybox.

She looked deep into his shiny,
brown-glass eyes. She kissed
the end of his leather nose.
And she remembered Big Dog.

*Never again,
Tedder!*

E
L

Low, Joseph

Don't drag your feet

DATE			

© THE BAKER & TAYLOR CO.